S. Campbell ● M. Di Russo

[baɪ]

S. Campbell ● M. Di Russo

[baɪ]

One farewell. *Two raconteurs.*

By
Shannon Campbell
Marcello Di Russo

S. Campbell • M. Di Russo

[baɪ]

Bye [baɪ] *(inform)* - used as a shortened form of goodbye to express farewell.

Bi- [baɪ] *prefix* - two; having two. Doubly, in two ways.

S. Campbell • M. Di Russo

[baɪ]

S. Campbell • M. Di Russo

INDEX

S. Campbell • M. Di Russo

I

The moment you start to appreciate the long path you took is a bigger reward than your final goal itself.

How much easier would be if I quit? But, how miserable would I be?

Sometimes, I think that everyone, right after they make some big and distinct decision, should capture that moment, and keep it with them. So, every time you feel this impulsive urge to quit, grab that moment back, and remember what brought you here.

Fuck no, I ain't no quitter.

I may relax sometimes, and sometimes I may freak out, especially in late November, I hate November, but I don't quit.

[baɪ]

Today I can say I'm happy.

A year or two ago, I could say that I wasn't
content with where I was, and I wanted so badly
to change it, and with time, it did. Things are
happening like they're supposed to. School is
what it is, I have great friends and my family is
happy and healthy.

This makes me really happy.

I'm so happy.

What we all need to do, is just live our lives, for
what it is. Try not to worry so much, because if
it's not going to kill you, you'll get over it. So,
enjoy what life hands you, even if it's a bag of
shit.

NYC

New York City, the place you could fall in love, get your heartbroken 20 times over. Lose everything, gain everything, become the richest and the poorest.

The City that breaks you to build you up.

The city that never sleeps. Bullshit!

New York City would sleep, trust me, it would, but it can't, or it decided not to. The main problem is in the numbers. Too many people, too big, too much. Funny, when you are not here, you think this city doesn't sleep.

I thought so too.

New York City doesn't sleep, it's too afraid to stop. It's frighten at the thought, so much so, it prefers to keep itself busy.

Once you stop what you're doing, you start to think, and your mind starts to spin so fast, you'll kill yourself with all those questions of "why?", the "for what?" NYC never sleeps, NYC never stops, it's too wild to decide to die.

Those crazy NYC nights. Vancouver Sleep Clinic, plays. Reminds me of Bon Iver.

I start to wonder of the future and what's to come. All the excitement, the ups, the downs, and the selfish moments. It reminds me how I need to be good to myself, love myself, respect myself and the woman I've become. The woman I am and the woman who's yet to come. Everything is and will be okay, so don't run, don't hide and just roll with the hard times and the good times will follow.

There will be people who come in and out of your life, some will impact you in a way, that you can't recover, or you think you won't, but you will.

Some will leave a stain that never leaves.

Some will come and go.

Some just for a moment.

But remember, in all of that, love the person you are; don't try to warp the perception or the voices telling you, this is what wins the game. The only thing that ever wins is being the player who is true to rules of themselves and their being.

The worries will subside one day, maybe. Could take months even years, but you'll have many more of these moments where you become one with the night sky, the stars and the moon. Your thoughts of worrying about, love, and career, Fun, no fun.

Nothing is more valid than your feelings. your wants and needs, no one else knows them better than you do. And it's okay to want something that's wrong on every level. Just never lose sight of what's important.

You, your sanity and your happiness, because at the end of it all you came alone and you leave alone.

When you break, you know where the pieces fell and you'll put them back together, one way or another, you may not have tackled it all, but you survived.

[baɪ]

TOUCH

-       Hey dude, tonight the girl I started to see may come to our place, are you there? Is it clean? LOL She is cool, maybe you ll see her tonite, even tho I hope we won't leave my room, you know what I am talking about! LOL later

-       My man!

I am scared the more time goes, the more I don't believe in what they call love. They told me, love is when you can't even think about living without her, or when your kid calls you daddy for the first time. When she holds your hand when you're feeling sick. I'm wondering, where is all of that? Why do they keep promising me that it's out there? The older I get, the more everything starts to look flat. I rarely get excited or happy.

This scares me a lot!

I hope I will never use you.

Believe me, I am a good person, and I would never hurt anybody, but I am scared. I'm scared that I may use you, to convince myself that love exists, and that I've now found this magical element that they keep talking about.

I don't want to hurt you, but, at the end of the day, what is this world if it's not what I perceive? I have seen the reality that surrounds me only through my eyes, and so I am the only filter between my understanding and the world and so, you are yours.

[baɪ]

Please, understand me, and use me, but don't tell me. Agree with me, it will be simple. We just need to lie to each other, and our truth will grow in time. Promise me, you will be on my side, but still, don't tell me.

*It's hard to know, exactly what you're looking
for. In some sense you'll never know or may
never find it. I know what I'm searching for.
I'm searching for a place for my heart to call
home. Whether it maybe making a bunch of
mistakes and trying to find the humor within
them or going on date after date to entertain
myself. Whatever it might be, I'm looking for an
adventure. Though within these experiences I'm
hoping for a solid ground to stand on.
As I grow, I've realized I want to be with
someone that feels like home.*

[baɪ]

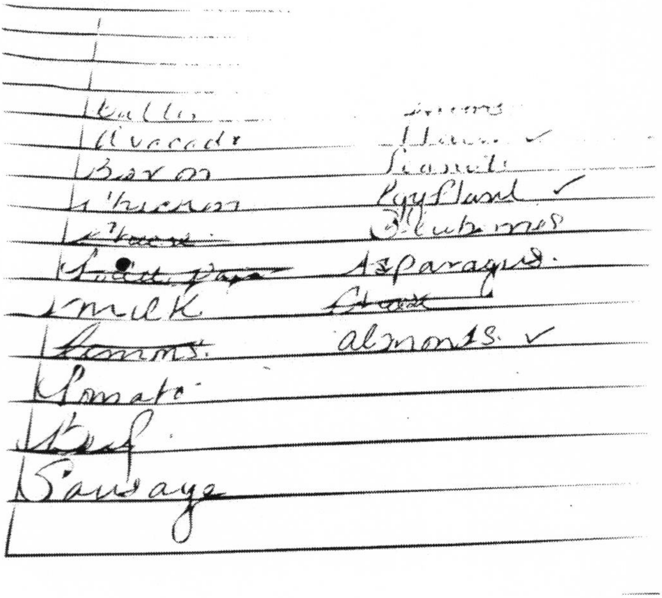
Avocado
Bacon
Chicken
milk
Tomato
Beef
Sausage
Asparagus.
almonts.

[baɪ]

IV

I can't wait for the day when someone looks at me like a miracle, like something they've waited for all their life.

I will meet a good man who loves me in 2018.

Is it her or myself? I've always had problems trying to understand how much I may like someone, or how much I may like the idea of satisfying my needs. We are social animals, we need to be with somebody, and I like this idea, and yes she is cool. But then, I think I have been single for a while, and this just started, and of course it is a good feeling. But why is it? It is her, or have I gotten to a place that I wished I've reached for such a long time? What will happen soon? Will I desire to go back to my single life?

I know, it is stupid to think too much and not enjoy the present, but I need to explore my thoughts, and I can't say the first thing that comes to mind. I have to be careful of myself, and for this innocent and beautiful creature who crossed my life.

[baɪ]

Pros

Nice to me.

Always make sure I'm taken care of, food and transportation

Nice friends

Listens to me when I'm talking about important things

Cons

Don't want one partner right now

Have sex with multiple people

Always on his phone

Good liar

Emotionally unavailable

Feel like I can only get his attention with sex

Parents may never accept me

Not affectionate

Needs

Someone who listens

Not on their phone all the time

Can talk about my day

Be there for me emotionally.

Spend time doing activities

Don't feel the need to use sex to get their

attention

Affectionate

[baɪ]

33

IM-
PERFECT-
IONS

She is the beautiful squared circle I've always been
looking for.

I will never stop to think that life is only about opportunities, and they're created by a perfect combination of timing and space.

Wise men say, it is all about being ready, because at one point, no matter how much talent you have, you will find that person who wants to see what you've got. That time arrives unexpected, and you got to be ready. Somebody out there likes you, but they just do not know you. So, be prepared, try to expose yourself as much as possible, but don't go crazy if it is not working out when you'd like it to happen: it is not on you, you can try hard, but you can't control it.

So, stop playing like a victim, and be ready.

[baɪ]

I'm not perfect and I'm never going to be.
I'm chaos. I'm unfiltered and sometimes I say
things that doesn't make sense: sometimes I
compile all the right things in my head, but for
some reason it comes out all wrong.
I do things the untraditional way, at times I do
things the wrong way though I know the right
way. I'm backwards, I get irritated and
miserable.
Sometimes quiet and don't to talk much. When
something is on my mind, I can't get it out
because I need to fix it before life goes on. I get
dramatic at times, but this is me.
I may never change much but with time these
traits will grow with me and become a better
part of me, so I'm not perfect: I'm imperfect in
every way possible.

THOSE CIRCLES

I was watching a video, and apparently, two different circles equal in size and color can appear different in size changing the size and distance of other figures surrounding them.

So true.

They say that you have to behave in a certain way to achieve that success. They say that you have to go out on Friday nights, and you shouldn't talk about philosophy in a bar; you want to be cool, don't you?

They talk too much.

They told us that we can't do that, that we don't talk like that to our partner, that it is insane to date exclusively in our late twenties living in this city. Isn't it?

They just talk too much.

They talk to me every time and ask me about my job, my favorite shows, my Tinder pics. They don't want to hear about philosophy, that for sure, I figured it out pretty quickly.

They talk way too much, but to the wrong person. They aren't talking to me, because I am not there anymore.

Yes, because my life is like a speed date, for a brief moment we talk to somebody in front of us, and then we move on, and the last person we talked to,

probably will never cross our life again. Every table
is a quick period of my life: the table of my
childhood, the table of my teenage years, the table
of that time I moved to college, and so on. I have
been sitting at so many tables and more is yet to
come. And what about them? Where are they?
How many are following me? How many keep
sitting next to me? Maybe my parents, and then?
Maybe you? How many words have they wasted,
because they were talking to the wrong person?
Talk to yourself, and keep it for yourself; you are
the only person who, for sure, will follow you
everywhere, at every table, no matter what: it's
worth it!

I wanna be wild, yet classy.

I wanna run wild around NYC, but still be taken seriously.

I wanna go crazy, but keep it together.

I wanna say fuck you, but still be friends.

I wanna lay in bed, but still get my work done.

I wanna kiss that guy in the bar and not feel ashamed.

I wanna say we are going out no questions asked.

I wanna walk with confidence and own it.

[baɪ]

LOVE SOMEBODY

Love is about giving parts of you, one didn't know exist. Going beyond reasonable doubt and being as vulnerable as any human being can be.

If only I had the courage to talk to you in person when I want, when I feel I need it. So much easier in front of a screen, or on paper. When I am with you I always get kind of distracted, and I always miss that perfect moment to tell you something I have been thinking for a long time.

Do you ever feel in the right space but at the wrong moment? Or vice versa?

Last night some words came out the wrong way, and it is never the way I imagined.

It is hard. I feel I am doing something wrong, and it is hard.

It feels so good now that everything is coming out from my mouth, I mean, my pen; but, once again, you're not here.

One day, one damn day! Maybe.

And if not?

I don't wanna think about it.

*I remember one line from that book it said
something like, happiness this profound is
frightening, because they're preparing to take
something from you. I remember because that's
what happened. Everything happened so fast.
We did everything fast: fight, love and sex. The
whole thing, It was thrusted at me like a dirty
sock after a long day, but it was that feel good
feeling; being able to wiggle my toes, it was like
that.*

*Then it was the time I got off the bus luggage in
hand. You told me how you only have a few
words. My mind kind of stopped, my lips started
to dry and do that thing where it gets that white
line. I was nervous.*

*You told me I was a "Good Girl" like you always
did. I wondered what that meant. I starred at
you with betrayal in my eyes. Hoping this could
change sooner rather than later but this time I
walked away. Head between my legs the tears*

fell to the carpet. He told me I needed to stop crying or else he wouldn't drive me home, I stopped, and the meter began.

I picked up the phone shaken from the disaster I thought would last. I screamed she said she thought someone had died. I cried she asked me to explain, but I couldn't. All she said was "cry".

It was 2 weeks later and you called. You wanted to see me to "chat" I said ok but I wasn't ok. You came and you're still here. And it started again. They say we become fools.

You lay there, you told me we are two friends who like each other a lot, that wasn't true. I lay my head on the pillow.

2 weeks later you wanted to chat. You said these things like it would get better or something like that, I'm not sure.

[baɪ]

[baɪ]

VIII

*We are all looking for something or someone to
get lost in.
Guess what?*

      Start with yourself and the rest will come.

              Amen

Ok, let's be clear, we are all selfish! Everybody is. You can do something huge for somebody else, but at the end you did it because you feel better when you receive the "thank you," or because you want to earn that fantastic seat in whatever incredible place you believe there is after death.

We are extremely selfish and the most generous people are the weakest one. Those who need a reward every time, they just take advantage of the rest of the world to satisfy their needs.

They demand validation, that's it.

How disgusting is that?

I am scared I am one of them though.

[baɪ]

I really enjoyed seeing you last night and was
happy to see you even though I was mad the
whole time. But, you're just the same person and
I don't think that's ever going to change. You
can never admit that I'm just a convenience, and
you keep me around until you feel you've met the
right girl. When you moved on, I'm left with
nothing and have to start over, and that's what
happened a couple months ago. I deserve to be
happy with someone who actually wants to be
with me and after these few years, I'm coming to
the realization that's not you.

You don't want to be in a relationship with me
and that's ok. You just use all my energy and
time and you don't love or care about me.
Because if you did or do you would let me be
happy with someone else.

You call me whenever you feel like you miss me,
but I think you just get lonely and want someone
there for your comfort and then you kick me to

the curb every chance you get. Like I said, I hope you stop calling me because you call me for all the wrong reasons.

[baɪ]

9

Running naked in a forest full of people acting like nothing is happening.

It would be unacceptable, but still

my prime desire.

S. Campbell • M. Di Russo

I wish I was one of those people who are incapable
of controlling their own impulses. We are animals,
we need to breath, to eat, to sleep, to fight and to
love. I don't know how it works for women, I have
never been one, but as a man, and please folks,
appreciate my honesty, I just need sex. When I
have it, my body feels better. Simple. We are
simple.

I am talking about sex and the desire of having
different companions, not lovers. I can separate my
body from my mind, and I don't know if, at this
point, it's a good or a bad thing.

I said mind, not heart.

It is a rational thought, fuck all the romantic
movies bullshits.

I won't go with anyone else, because I've learned
how to respect you, and I don't want to hurt you.
But only if you can understand, and only if you
could go with somebody else, I would sleep with so
many people, just for the desire to explore
something different.

58

[baɪ]

I love your body, and I feel the fire when you undress in front of me, when you hug me from behind, when you touch me, when you scratch my back with your nails. But still, I want to see, smell and touch something different from you.
If only you would understand and accept this...
Would that be real proof of love? You let me go, and me always coming back to you.

These are the rules! You don't get to just show up over here to get laid whenever it's convenient for you. it's not convenient for me not anymore. And I get it now. This is not me trying to make you feel sorry for me. It's your lost anyway. This is going nowhere, you've had intentions of moving on and I was always just convenience for you. Yes, maybe I did still like having you around again but, it's obvious that it can't happen anymore because trying to force someone's hand never yields positive outcome.

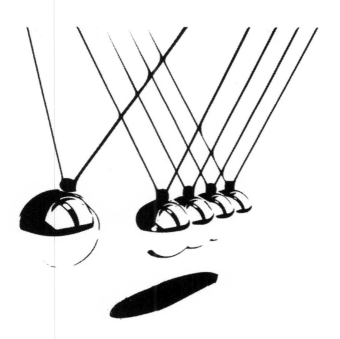

I LOVE
I HATE
I DON'T

Why do we think primarily in black and white
when this life is only about shades of grey?

Hi, I am sorry for yesterday but, please, don't ask me if I love you, don't do it again. Nothing against you, but you know what I think about it. I don't name feelings, it is quite impossible for me. How can you possibly describe and give a name to something so personal? How could I possibly, only with my words, make someone else understand the way I feel?

"Love" is just a word of void, like "hate", or "fear", or whatever.

I speak through my actions.

Yes, I like spending time with you, I smile every time I see your text notifications pop up on my phone screen. I listen to you, I cook for you, I want to make you smile and much more. Is this love? Don't ask me.

But please just understand that I am here for you.

[baɪ]

There's not much to say to the person that makes you happy other than thank you, for making me happy on my worst of days, and for making me happier on my best of days.

Never forget to enjoy the simplest things in life. It's easy sometimes to miss out on the important moments, because we are busy dwelling on meaningless matters. So remember live your life, have some fun, enjoy the simplicity and make the best of it.

When you feel like everything is crumbling and you want to give up, remember that you are a strong person and your going to conquer what it is you came for. Enjoy what's in front of you, discover a new you, and don't be afraid to seek out the unknown. Explore life because it's all we have. There will never be a time ever again for you to say "you know what I did for the first time yesterday." You only have so many chances to say that, so why waste it thinking what if?

because what if's won't bring back tomorrow.
Yesterday was yesterday, today is today and so it
will be.

[baɪ]

I hate it when you lecture me

I hate it when you tell me I'm wrong

I hate it when you talk to me as if you're

quizzing me and I feel stupid

But I love it when you text me

I love it when I refuse to do anything around 10

because I'm anticipating your call

I love it when you kiss my cheek

I love it when you slide your palm down my hand

just to reach mine

I love it when you pinch my cheek

I love it when you grab my butt

I love it when you laugh at my jokes and weird

phrase

I love it when you say my name

I love the things I'm yet to love

NYC II

Symptoms of NYC

Relationships

Loneliness

Struggling professional and personally

Is there anybody who cares about what I am doing?

Can somebody tell me if I'm doing a good job?

What the hell am I doing here?

Since I moved here, day after day I feel smaller and smaller in this ocean, but a much bigger fish than yesterday. I feel I am a man now; I do accept my responsibilities, and I want to play!

However, so many times I feel lost, and nobody cares.

[baɪ]

*When you're in an Uber and didn't even know
someone was getting picked up and then, a tug at
the door so hard you think you're getting robbed.
Then someone gets in the car and proceed to play
their Instagram feed on speaker for everyone in
NYC to enjoy. I tell yah though, very smart,
started to inform me about the new tax reform
and Net Neutrality.*

FINDING EACH OTHER

Never measure feelings with time when it comes
to matters of the heart, time means nothing.
                    Your heart does not measure
                              feelings in time.

It is the first time I am thinking about ending something with someone I like, because I feel it would be better for my future.

Yes, time will heal, but why stop right now? Every time I've heard of somebody hurting themselves only because "it will be better for me although I don't want it", I always thought, it's stupid and wrong.

I need to admit, now I can understand better what they meant. The past is only a reference, the future will be shaped by today's decisions, so, if it's good now, don't let it go!

Don't be a pussy!

Face the fact, she is different from everyone else, and she dragged you all the way inside this situation, and you agreed with that. Stop comparing her with your past women, she is different.

Grow up!

She got you, somehow, no further explanations needed.

[baɪ]

Tell her. Be honest.

Don't waste time now, it will lead you to many

future regrets. The time you acted like an

emotional teenager is gone.

Be a man!

You ever feel like you're looking for something in life you're never going to find. It's like this never ending search, a search for the unknown. Everyday you try to figure out what this thing could be, maybe there will be a sign somewhere, someone to tell you what direction to take. Then you think, I don't want to take the wrong direction or I won't find it. The only thing, I don't even know what i'm looking for or where to start. I guess what I have to do is stop searching, like they say: once you stop searching, whatever it is will find you.

[baɪ]

REFLECTIONS

Trust the proverbs, trust the older people, they
have been around longer than you!
Put your ego down, moron!

REFLECTIONS

Trust the proverbs, trust the older people, they
have been around longer than you!

Put your ego down, moron!

Extremes are bad and dangerous. Even the most healthy and beautiful thing you can think of, if it's "too much" it's bad. "Too" generous and kind, equal, they will take advantage because you don't show balls. "Too much" love, equal, boring!

How can you appreciate something if you don't know the feeling of missing it? I am scared that we are becoming a habit, and I am scared I don't remember how it feels without you.

It is hard fighting for you now.

It is sad.

I am so sorry.

[baɪ]

It's hard to navigate our way through this thing
called life. It can be pleasant at times, but other
times it hands us shit on a platter. They say its
what you turn the negative into, but we all know
nothing good can come from shit.
Just enjoy it.
What I'm trying to say is: you're going to have
good days and bad ones. At times you may feel
you're on top, other times you feel like you're
being kicked around. But know that it doesn't
last forever; we may not have it all figured out,
but you will its never too late.

"For what it's worth it's never too late"
F. Scott Fitzgerald

XIV

It's this unexplainable feeling, my soul feels empty. Nothing fill my thoughts, I'm in a limbo. How do I stop this floating feeling? This lifeless feeling?

What does it mean?

You will be fine, you will. I am sure.

I really can't express this feeling; I am sad it is going to happen, but I can't wait to move on. It will be better for both of us.

You will be fine, and that is what really matters. I can't understand how people did not see what a beautiful person you are, and you deserve the best. I am not the best for you.

It may sound like the classic excuse to leave you, but it is not, it is true. I am not leaving you, it's your brightness and your charisma that makes me feel unworthy.

Our incompatibility are leaving me.

How much time I made you waste because of me? How much energy you could have spent for yourself instead that for us and this endless pain? We just don't work, and that's ok. It is ok because you will be fine; you will be great, let the time do its job, and please forgive me.

I need your effort, I am weak, I can't separate from you, I need you to leave. It may sound weird, but it

[baɪ]

is just me showing all my impotence. You are

better than me, so I am here to ask you for the last

effort, please leave.

Act on it or forget it.

That time when we were on the bus, and it hit a bump the wheel came off. Then there was the other time we stood by a donut shop and you said something like, leave or something or the other. It was me or that.
I wasn't ready.
We got to your apartment, I sat on the couch. This unfamiliar room, not much room between each piece of furniture, one after the other lined the walls. You told me you were sorry for the way you spoke to me. I had these puppy dog eyes lost among all the chaos of us. I walked into the bedroom, my eye ran from one corner to the other, seems like you didn't clean often.
You came in and hug me from behind, we undress. We laid in the bed while you told me how you're happy that I didn't walk away. Though I knew that I should. I felt hopeless. But at the same time happy we were still one in our chaos.
I was happy.

[baɪ]

[baɪ] - [baɪ]

- *Hey… I just want to let you know that I wish you the best. I just want to end things on a good note. I don't hate you and I don't want to yell and scream at you anymore. We weren't always good to each other at times, but at some point you made me really happy. I still love and care about you, but I can't be your friend right now maybe not even in five months or ever. I want you to know that I hope everything that you want and need in life, and everything you're dealing with, I hope it all works out for you.*

[baɪ]

-       I got your text, thank you.
BYE, love you.

[baɪ]

[baɪ]

S. Campbell • M. Di Russo

[baɪ]

S. Campbell • M. Di Russo

[baɪ]

17905988R00061

Made in the USA
Middletown, DE
05 December 2018